1001 DAD JOKES
COMPLETE EDITION

M C JEPSEN

CAPTIVA GREEN PUBLISHING

Published by Captiva Green Publishing © 2020.

First Edition.

Cover images by Freepik.com
Cover and book design, production, and editing by Captiva Green Publishing

For Fun.

Contents

1001 DAD JOKES: COMPLETE EDITION

VOLUME I

CHAPTER 1

Why did Stalin only write in lowercase?
He didn't like capitalism.

§

My son claims that he identifies as an
ancient Greek string instrument.
Frankly, I think he's a lyre.

§

Why did the cowboy get a dachshund?
Someone told him to get along little doggie.

§

Would anyone be interested in being my companion?
Asking for a friend.

§

I used to detest my job hanging from the ceiling,
blowing air at people. Now I'm a big fan.

§

The best paper towels and toilet paper are truly tearable.

§

In the face of mounting bills after losing my job,
I decided to cut out the middle of our last loaf of bread.
At that point, I could make ends meet.

§

How do you organize a space party?
You planet.

§

I accidentally swallowed a bunch of Scrabble tiles.
My next trip to the bathroom could spell disaster.

§

My colleagues at work have given me
the nickname 'Mr. Compromise.'
It's not my first choice, but I'm ok with it.

Why did the mountain hate the beach?
He wasn't shore.

§

My wife kicked me out of the house because of
my bad Schwarzenegger impressions.
But don't worry, I will return.

§

What do you call bears with no ears?
B.

§

Why can't two elephants go swimming at the same time?
Because they only have one pair of trunks.

§

Why was the lettuce ultimately convicted at trial?
It didn't romaine silent.

§

When I was young, my dad used to tear up
the last page of all my comic books
and never told me why.
I had to draw my own conclusions.

§

Algebra is easy, I can deal with trigonometry,
and I'll struggle through calculus.
But graphing is where I draw the line.

§

The German language has a word for everything.
That is alles.

§

My uncle purchased a cherry and a microphone.
He bought a bing, bought a boom.

§

Today, I saw someone in the cardio section put a water bottle
in the Pringles holder on the treadmill.

§

My dog only responds to commands in Spanish.
He's a Cocker Español.

What do you call a poodle in the summer?
A hot dog, and in the winter it's a chili dog.

§

My wife was upset that I bought the wrong cheddar and
promptly slammed it on the table.
I said: "Well, that's mature."

§

Not to brag, but I already have a date for Valentine's Day.
February 14th.

§

What do you do if you find a space man?
Park your car.

§

I tried the new Bible-themed restaurant called
'The Lord Giveth.'
They also do take away.

§

I'm sad that my Samsung printer stopped working today.
It was like a Brother to me.

§

Spring has finally arrived.
I'm so excited that I wet my plants.

§

Last night, I had the craziest dream that I wrote
Lord of the Rings.
I must have been Tolkien in my sleep.

§

During prenatal class,
I was asked if I had ever been present for a birth.
I replied, "Yes, once." I was then asked to describe it.
I said, "It was dark, then suddenly very bright."

§

I was so bored that I read six pages of the dictionary.
I learned next to nothing.

CHAPTER 2

Why did the dad tell the joke?
To get to the other sigh.

§

Did you hear that the bathroom
at the doughnut shop was vandalized?
The police have nothing to go on.

§

What do you call a hen who counts her eggs before they hatch?
A foolish mathemachicken.

§

What happens when you think you're on a porch,
but you're actually not?
The gazebo effect.

§

I called the casino to ask why the
deck of cards I ordered hadn't arrived.
They assured me they were dealing with it.

§

My calculator broke today.
I can't count on it anymore.

§

I let my manager know I needed a raise as I was
getting a lot of calls from three companies.
My boss asked:
"Can you share which are after you?"
"Cable, electric, and gas," I said.

§

Did you know that many
mental institutions have hiking trails?
Some are absolutely full of psychopaths.

§

Someone asked if I had heard of Pavlov's dog.
I told her it rang a bell.

My wife asked for a sharper knife.
The other one just wasn't cutting it.

§

I rescued a dog that once belonged to a blacksmith.
The first thing he did when I brought him home
was make a bolt for the door.

§

Why did the teacher wear sunglasses to school?
Because her students were so bright.

§

My dog used to chase people on a bike often.
It got so bad I had to take his bike away.

§

I saw my nephew after a year and said,
"Wow! You must have grown a foot since I saw you last."
He said, "Nope. Still only have the two."

§

What should Shrek wear when he gets sweaty?
Deogreant.

§

I have a fear of speed bumps.
I'm slowly getting over it.

§

Why did Frosty move in with his friends?
So he wouldn't feel so ice-olated.

§

What do you call an artist who's also a street racer?
Vincent Van Go!

§

Insurance companies are warning campers
that if their tent is stolen during the night,
they won't be covered.

§

I changed my iPod's name to 'Titanic' in iTunes.
It's syncing now.

When I was young, I wondered where the sun went at night.
Then it dawned on me.

§

I hate it when you sincerely compliment someone's mustache
and suddenly she's not your friend anymore.

§

My bank called to let me know I had an outstanding balance.
I said, "Thank you,
I was a star gymnast in high school," and hung up.

§

My neighbors listen to really good music,
whether they like it or not.

§

Face is a four letter word, but preface is a foreword letter.

§

Did you hear about the guy who caught himself on the railing
before falling down the airport steps?
He missed the flight.

§

My grandfather was an abacus salesman in 1960s.
He was part of the counter culture.

§

My wife tripped and dropped the
basket of clothes she had freshly ironed.
I watched it all unfold.

§

I was going to throw away all of my old spices.
But it seemed like a waste of thyme.

§

Did you see the woman that was walking down the street
and turned into a café?

§

I'm really proud of my friend's
collection of stage production equipment.
Props to her.

CHAPTER 3

Once, I drank some food coloring.
I dyed a little inside.

§

I think I should learn sign language.
It's very handy.

§

Man calls his wife's OBGYN and says,
"It's time, we need your help!"
The nurse says, "Calm down. Is this her first child?"
He replies, "No! This is her husband!"

§

Which farm animal is most likely to be hit by a car?
The chicken.
It always seems to be crossing the road.

§

Who are the most boring people?
Jen, Eric.

§

My most memorable
elementary school teacher was Ms. Turtle.
Funny name, but she tortoise well.

§

Hey officer, how did the hackers escape?
"No idea, they just ransomware."

§

I was afraid that I broke my sewing machine.
It seams fine now.

§

Why did the doctor quit his practice to find a new career?
He lost his patience.

§

My doctor advised that I avoid all fast food.
Unfortunately, snails don't taste very good.

When I realized the play was a dud,
I resigned from the stage design team.
I left without making a scene.

§

True fact: The fastest car in the world
is faster than the rest of the cars.

§

Did you hear about the support website for
depressed tennis players?
The servers are currently down.

§

A king needed to name his soldiers.
Queen: "I'm going to bed."
King: "But I need a name for my soldiers."
Queen: "K, night."
King: "Honey, you're a genius!"

§

What do you call fake potatoes?
Imitaters.

§

I relabeled the jars in our spice rack.
I haven't gotten into trouble with my wife just yet,
but the thyme is cumin.

§

According to a recent study,
nine out of ten people who are afraid of hurdles
never get over it.

§

Had an argument with my chiropractor about my posture.
I now stand corrected.

§

Do you know about the man who had a second job
closing the casing tubes of sausage links?
He made meat ends to make ends meet.

§

Our letter carrier never gets the humor in my best jokes.
I guess the key to a good mailman joke is the delivery.

I was fired from my last job even though I always gave 100%.
Apparently that's not how you grade exams.

§

What do you call an animal that hoards all the dirt?
A groundhog.

§

My cat threw up on the carpet.
I don't think he's feline well.

§

What did one casket say to the other?
"That you coughin'?"

§

This spring, my friend finished a graduate program in archeology;
I asked why she pursued this career path.
She said she digs the past.

§

A friend at a party dressed up as a Band-Aid for Halloween.
It looked hard to pull off.

§

You'd think a snail would be faster without a shell.
Turns out it's more sluggish.

§

What do you call a hen staring at lettuce and croutons?
Chicken sees a salad.

§

What washes up on tiny beaches?
Microwaves.

§

I've been trying to come up with a joke related to sewing.
If only I had some material.

§

What do you call a royal mummy with a sore throat?
Not sure. Sir Cough, I guess?

CHAPTER 4

When my grandfather was ill, we rubbed lard on his back.
He went downhill quite quickly after that.

§

I saw a baguette in a cage during my last trip to the zoo.
The zookeeper told me it was bread in captivity.

§

What's the difference between bird flu and swine flu?
One's cured with tweetment, the other, oinkment.

§

I was going to add jokes about penguins to my routine
until I realized they won't fly.

§

What do goats and cows tell each other at bedtime?
Dairy tales.

§

My girlfriend is obsessed with roofing tools
so I gave her an ultimatum:
it's either me or the tools.
She chose the latter.

§

Today I raced a Frenchman and easily beat him.
Nice guys finish last.

§

Have you seen the Disney movie about an
ugly DJ in a small club somewhere in Alsace?
Beauty and the Beats.

§

I stopped looking for my watch.
I just couldn't find the time.

§

I'm collecting signatures to secure funding for new slides
at our neighborhood playground.
Support for the issue is declining rapidly.

I wrote a joke about blowing my nose.
I thought it would be funny but it's snot.

§

What do you call a timely dinosaur?
A prontosaurus.

§

Granddad: "Don't come in here, I just passed a silent one."
Grandmom: "Honey, I think you need a new battery in your
hearing aid."

§

My girlfriend poked me in the eyes.
I stopped seeing her for a little while.

§

How do you get a farm girl to like you?
A tractor.

§

I was held up on the street for my toothbrush.
The robber said: hand it over, Oral-B mad.

§

Did you know that Captain Kirk has three ears?
A left ear, a right ear, and a final frontier.

§

When I came to after getting hit by a truck,
I was shocked to discover my fingers were broken.
It was hard to grasp.

§

Our wedding was so beautiful, even the cake was in tiers.

§

What kind of bagel do pilots like?
Plain.

§

Today I saw twin pandas.
I thought, "That bears repeating."

§

A friend of mine jumped off a bridge in Paris.
Guy was in Seine.

I had to stop using laxatives after
eating at the Bavarian restaurant.
They really bring out the wurst in me.

§

What do you call parasites that suck cleaning chemicals?
Bleeches.

§

Why does the IRS audit seafood restaurants so often?
Something in their kitchens is always a bit fishy.

§

I started my first herb garden;
each plant is sorted alphabetically.
My wife asked me, with work and the kids, how I find the time.
I said, easy, it's right next to the sage.

§

People who can't tell the difference between
etymology and entomology bug me beyond words.

§

I asked my brother why he only
uses his superpowers on my daughters.
He told me he only has telekinesis, not telekinephews.

§

Did you hear about the lawyer who forgot his bag in court?
It was a brief case.

§

What did the cowboy say at his second rodeo?
This ain't my first rodeo.

§

How many balls of lint would it take to reach the moon?
One, but it would need to be very large.

§

I refused to accept that my dad was stealing
from his job with the highway commission.
However, when I got home the signs were all there.

CHAPTER 5

Two satellites got married.
The wedding was out of this world
and the reception was amazing.

§

What's the difference between a jeweler and a jailer?
One sells watches, while the other watches cells.

§

I heard a kid scattered his scrabble letters
on the road as he fell off his bike.
At least that's the word on the street.

§

Why don't you find hippos hiding in trees?
Because they're really good at it.

§

I received thousands of letters in the mail today.
That's the last time I order a dictionary from Ikea.

§

What do Santa's elves listen to while they work?
Wrap music.

§

What language did the first person in Portugal speak?
Portugoose.

§

Our director is going to fire the employee
with the worst posture.
I have a hunch, it might be me.

§

I think I'm allergic to the gym.
Whenever I'm there, I get sweaty, my face turns red,
my heart beats rapidly, and my breathing is short.

§

A man sued an airline company after they lost his luggage.
Sadly, he lost his case.

What is the least spoken language in the world?
Sign language.

§

Did you hear about the snowman that ran away from home?
Apparently, the trail went cold.

§

I own a pencil that once belonged to William Shakespeare.
The problem is that he chewed it a lot.
I can't tell if it's 2B or not 2B.

§

Accordion to a recent survey,
replacing words with the names of musical instruments
often goes undetected.

§

An Englishman, an Irishman, and a Scotsman walk into a bar.
The barman asks: "Is this a joke?"

§

What do you call a cow with no legs?
Ground beef.

§

As I put my car in reverse,
I thought to myself, this takes me back.

§

My son asked what 'inexplicable' means.
I told him it's hard to explain.

§

My wife showed me her mother's quilts and
asked which I preferred.
I told her I'd rather not make a blanket judgment.

§

My son managed to bake something on his first try.
It was a piece of cake.

§

If money doesn't grow on trees,
why do banks have branches?

This girl and I are getting serious.
We went to see the new Batman movie on our ninth date.
Our relationship has been: dinner, dinner, dinner, dinner,
dinner, dinner, dinner, dinner, Batman.

§

Did you know they banned round hay bales?
The horses weren't getting a square meal.

§

Did you hear about the haunted tractor?
It was rumbling down a country road
when it turned into a field.

§

Ladies, if your boyfriend asks for
matador equipment for his birthday,
it's big red flag.

§

What's a pirate's favorite Apple product?
The iPatch.

§

My wife wanted me to skip
my friend's BBQ to go to the theater.
I'm afraid it would have been a big missed-steak.

§

Greek mythology was never my strong suit while in school.
You could say it was my Achilles elbow.

§

Why is a tree a better deterrent than a guard dog?
It has more bark.

§

After my annual physical, my doctor prescribed a
pill I'll have to take daily for the rest of my life.
The bottle only had four pills.

§

The police arrested two men:
one for drinking battery acid,
and the other for eating fire crackers.
They charged one and let the other off.

CHAPTER 6

During high school, we lived on a houseboat and
I fell in love with the girl next door.
Eventually, we drifted apart.

§

I took my friend's favorite board game without him noticing.
He doesn't have a clue.

§

I wanted to attend the seminar on vomit control.
Unfortunately, something came up.

§

The big used car dealership in town recently doubled its size.
It can offer a whole lot more.

§

How do people in Star Trek tolerate high speeds?
They Klingon to something.

§

My earliest childhood memory is visiting
the optometrist and getting my glasses.
Life before that was a blur.

§

Guys, this is so sad.
The water boiled.
It shall be mist.

§

Sometimes I tell dad jokes.
Sometimes he even laughs at them.

§

Where do Audis go when they retire?
The old Volks home.

§

Did you hear about the pizza parlor that
reopened as a butcher shop?
The owner flips each cut in the air like dough.
The steaks have never been higher.

What does blackened clownfish taste like?
It probably tastes a little funny.

§

To all the people out there suffering with paranoia:
remember, you're not alone.

§

What's E.T. short for?
Because he has little legs.

§

Did you hear about the sad puppy that only eats cantaloupe?
He's a little melon collie.

§

I think my wife is changing my son's diaper too often.
The box says they are good for up to 16 pounds.

§

I lost my job as a bank teller.
When an older woman asked me to check her balance,
I pushed her over.

§

My therapist told me my narcissism
causes me to misread social situations.
I'm pretty sure she was flirting with me.

§

How did the picture end up in jail?
It was framed.

§

You haven't heard the joke about the three deep holes?
Well, well, well.

§

Did you see the newest magazine for
bookworms who enjoy oil paint jokes?
It's called Readers Dye Jest.

§

My wife threw me out of the house
because I'm obsessed with talking like a news anchor.
More on that after the break.

What is most birds' favorite drink?
Nest-café.

§

I turned in my project on gingivitis just in time.
I made it by the skin of my teeth.

§

A man showed up for a duel armed only with a pencil and paper.
He proceeded to draw his weapon.

§

What ever happened to the stuttering prisoner?
He could never finish his sentence.

§

Why was the man afraid of a bra?
He knew it was a booby trap.

§

Why did the scarecrow win an award?
He was outstanding in his field.

§

I asked a beekeeper for a dozen bees.
He counted out thirteen and handed them over.
"You've given me one too many," I said.
"That one's a freebie."

§

My son won't eat Atlantic haddock or lobster.
He has Pacific taste in seafood.

§

I called IT because music was coming out of the printer.
They told me it's just jammin' again.

§

Did you know iTunes is selling a track for just forty-five cents?
It's a new song by 50cent featuring Nickelback.

CHAPTER 7

To make extra money, our professor requires all of his students
to buy his book at the beginning of the term.
It's textbook economics.

§

A young karate champion joined the military.
The first time he saluted his CO, he had a headache for weeks.

§

Where do bass keep their money?
At the river bank.

§

I asked Melissa why she married me.
"Honey, because you're so funny!"
I questioned, "I thought it's because I'm smart and attractive?"
She replied, "See? You're hilarious!"

§

The top five reasons for procrastination:
1) boredom 2) work ethic.

§

Did you hear about the actor that literally broke a leg on stage?
Don't worry; he's still in the cast.

§

What do you get when the sun bends over
very late in the evening?
The crack of dawn.

§

Found a new bread recipe where you don't have to
get your hands dirty mixing the dough.
It is kneadless, to say.

§

Did you hear about the amphibious musicians?
Their music is ribbiting.

§

I had a hard time finding rubber snakes at the toy store.
Eventually, I found them in the rept-aisle.

Why do people rarely starve in the desert?
Because of all the sand which is there.

§

What do you call a four foot six psychic that escaped from prison?
A small medium at large.

§

An otter was swimming quickly upriver
when it suddenly ran into a wall.
After being startled, it looked at the wall and said "Dam!"

§

Someone stole the soap from the bathroom again.
The culprit made a clean get away.

§

Take my advice, do not inhale poisonous gases.
You may very well sulfur the consequences.

§

Today I bumped into the guy who sold me a globe.
It's a small world.

§

How many narcissists does it take to change a light bulb?
One.
She holds it up and the world revolves around her.

§

A vegan said to me, "People who sell meat are disgusting!"
I said, "People who sell fruits and vegetables are grocer."

§

Justice is best served cold.
If it was served warm, it would be just water.

§

How to fall down a staircase, a step by step guide:
Step 1. Step 2. Step 3. Step 4. Step 5. Step 6.

§

A lamb, a drum, and a snake fell off a cliff. Baa-Dumm-Tss

§

What happens when you throw a Finnish sailor overboard?
Helsinki.

Within minutes, the detectives at the scene
discovered the murder weapon, still bloody.
It was a brief case.

§

What did the fish monger say to the magician?
Pick a cod, any cod.

§

I wanted to tell a long joke about a dog getting fixed.
But the owner only wanted a quick snippet.

§

What did the zero say to the ten?
How did you find the one?

§

Why are North Koreans the best at geometry?
Because they have a Supreme Ruler.

§

Started work on a plane that used stilts instead of wings.
The project had a ton of support but never took off.

§

Doctor: "I will be delivering your baby."
Parents: "We'd prefer he keep his liver, please."

§

I heard the greatest joke about drills.
Wait, never mind, it was a dull bit.

§

As a high schooler, I was offered a job in a monastery laundry.
My parents said no way.
They didn't want me picking up dirty habits.

§

What I if told you... You read the joke wrong.

CHAPTER 8

Everyone in our reggae band agreed
we had to fire the triangle player.
It was just one ting after another with him.

§

What happened when the cow tried to
jump the barbed wire fence?
Utter destruction.

§

Why does the alphabet drop to 25 letters every December?
Noel.

§

I entered ten of my best puns into a competition
to see if any would win.
No pun in ten did.

§

I'd like to thank, you, student loans,
for getting me through college.
I don't think I'll ever be able to repay you.

§

I was in my doctor's office when someone started yelling:
"Typhoid! Tetanus! Measles!"
I asked the nurse what was going on.
She told me that the doctor likes to call the shots.

§

My wife hates pizza jokes.
Most of them are too cheesy.

§

I don't trust caricature artists.
Their work is a little too sketchy.

§

A median and a mode walk into a bar.
The bartender says,
"I'm glad you ditched your friend. He's mean."

Three conspiracy theorists walk into a bar.
You can't tell me that's just a coincidence.

§

Fun fact: prior to achieving immense popularity
with "Sweet Caroline,"
Neil Diamond was called Neil Carbon.
Ultimately, the pressure got to him.

§

When my dear oma died, she was cremated.
I had her ashes placed in a trophy that read:
"World's Best Grandma."
She urned it.

§

My job as a freight elevator repairman has its ups and downs.

§

A Buddhist monk walks up to a
hot dog vendor and says:
"Make me one with everything."

§

What did the toucan say to the cashier
when she bought a tube of lipstick?
Can you put it on my bill?

§

What do vegetarian zombies say?
Grrrrrainnnnnssss.

§

An old man driving home hears an alert:
"Breaking news: One car going the wrong way on Main Street.
Drivers, be careful."
Looking around, he says:
"One? There are hundreds!"

§

What do you call a happy rabbit?
A hoptimist.

§

"Oh my, you must have grown a foot since I last saw you!"
[Doctor, seeing a patient after visiting Chernobyl].

What did the pirate tell his friends when he turned 80?
Aye matey.

§

What happens if your band has two drummers?
There will be repercussions.

§

What was the bee's reaction when it won the lottery?
It was just buzzing.

§

How do you cut the ocean in half?
With a seasaw.

§

How does a crazy person find their way out of the wilderness?
They just follow the pyscho path.

§

What do you call a wedding between two communists?
A Soviet union.

§

My wife thinks we should stop buying so much
processed deli meat from the grocer.
I agreed; we should quit cold turkey.

§

Do you know what's really odd?
Numbers not divisible by two.

§

How do you make an egg laugh?
You tell it a funny yolk.
It really cracks them up.

§

You may have seen the email going around about canned meats.
Don't open it, it's spam.

§

I'm really hoping to sell my broken bike tire pump.
But really, no pressure, guys.

§

My daughter picked up a piece of fruit and asked, "Is this a pear?"
"No," I replied, "There's only one."

VOLUME II

CHAPTER 9

Did you make the opening of the new store that only sells
organic doughnuts, bagels, and Swiss cheese?
They call it Hole Foods.

§

My daughters... just like their mother.
I wish they liked their father too.

§

I dreamed about swimming in an ocean of orange soda last night.
It took a while to realize it was a Fanta sea.

§

What's the difference between a doctor and God?
God doesn't think he's a doctor.

§

Why was the stadium so cool and windy?
It was filled with fans.

§

How many apples grow on trees?
All of them.

§

The rotation of the earth really makes my day.

§

Grounded by snow, I ate breakfast at the airport.
My eggs came on a shiny metal plate, so I asked why.
The waitress explained:
"It's Christmas and there's no plates like chrome for the
hollandaise."

§

I went to the therapist after my phone died.
I just needed an outlet.

My friend asked if I had a haircut.
I told her no, of course not, I got them all cut.

§

When do transformers do most of their online shopping?
Optimus Prime Day.

§

We had a great joke about unrefined oil,
but it would probably have tanked.
It's a little too crude.

§

Gambling addiction hotlines would do so much better if
every seventh caller was a winner.

§

If America changed from pounds to kilograms overnight,
it would create mass confusion.

§

I'd like to thank my legs for supporting me,
my arms for staying at my side,
and my fingers because I can always count on them.

§

Do you know about the newly uncovered
secret society of beverages?
They call themselves the Illuminatea.

§

This week, someone knocked on my door soliciting donations
for a neighborhood swimming pool.
I told him of course, and offered a bottle of water.

§

Have you heard of whiteboards?
They're a pretty remarkable invention.

§

In what state does the Missouri river flow?
Liquid.

§

A friend of mine asked me to adopt two young calves.
Naturally, I agreed. What can I say?
I'm always willing to raise the steaks.

Why weren't the vultures allowed to board their flight?
They had too many carrions.

§

What's the best part about living in Switzerland?
It's hard to say, but the flag is a big plus.

§

Why does Sherlock Holmes love Mexican restaurants?
They give him good case ideas.

§

I'm not a fan of Russian dolls.
They're so full of themselves.

§

Have you heard of that new pirate movie?
It's rated arrrghhh.

§

What do you call the Italian technician at the
Large Hadron Collider who makes prosecco on weekends?
A fizzycist.

§

A convict escaped from prison wearing paper towel shorts.
He now has a bounty on his head and his butt.

§

I gave up assembling the last part on my new bike.
I just couldn't handle it.

§

What are a communist's favorite units of time?
Hours.

§

I get agitated whenever I hear A, E, I, O, or U.
Turns out I have irritable vowel syndrome.

§

Someone stole a full case of Red Bull from my store.
I don't know how they can sleep at night.

CHAPTER 10

I only gamble on the top floor of casinos.
My odds are better when I roll high.

§

I asked a hundred women which shampoo they preferred.
Their number one answer was: How did you get in here?

§

What is the difference between
ignorance, apathy, and ambivalence?
I don't know and I don't care one way or the other.

§

As I suspected, someone has been adding clay to my garden.
The plot thickens.

§

Why did the tennis player die alone despite many suitors?
Love meant nothing to her.

§

My grandfather woke up before dawn every day to go sailing.
When I asked him why so early,
he told me: "The schooner, the better!"

§

Someone stole my mood ring.
I'm not sure how I feel about it.

§

What do you call a boat full of high school graduates?
A scholarship.

§

Why couldn't Usain Bolt listen to music while running?
He kept breaking the record.

§

I had an amazing childhood;
my dad used to roll us down hills in tires.
Those were Goodyears.

Why was the orange juice factory worker fired?
He couldn't concentrate.

§

I asked my astronomer neighbor if he'd like some veggie pizza.
He said he'd prefer something meteor.

§

How did the farmer find his wife?
He tractor down.

§

I asked my wife if she'd like to celebrate our anniversary
in the south of France.
She said sure, we have nothing Toulouse.

§

My girlfriend and I met for dinner after work.
After a while, I whispered "I love you."
She asked "Is that you or the beer talking?"
I answered "It's me talking to the beer."

§

Why did the ram jump over the cliff?
He didn't see the ewe turn.

§

I heard that parallel lines have a lot in common.
It's too bad they never meet.

§

I've opened a barber shop for rabbits.
We only do hare cuts.

§

A man went to a library for a book about lubricants.
The librarian showed him the non-friction section.

§

Do you remember the sitcom about airplanes that never took off?
The pilot was terrible.

§

What is the fastest liquid on earth?
Running water.

A T. rex walks into a vegan restaurant and is greeted by
someone who said she knew him.
He had never met herbivore.

§

I've never liked the study of tunnel-making.
It's boring.

§

A bottle of Coke fell out of the fridge and onto my toes.
I'm fortunate it was a soft drink.

§

I saw an ad for burial plots, and thought to myself,
this is the last thing I need.

§

I felt pretty sick after drinking milk with cream.
My stomach was churning for a while,
but now it's butter.

§

Have you ever tried blindfolded archery?
You don't know what you're missing.

§

I invented beach footwear for people with one leg.
It was a flop.

§

How do percussionists get their seafood?
They castanet.

§

You want to know the way to my heart?
A scalpel and a bone saw.

§

What do you call a snake building its own home?
A boa constructor.

CHAPTER 11

Two hungry travelers lost in the desert see a bacon shrub.
One makes a run for it and gets caught up in a net.
He yells to his friend:
"Stop! It's not a bacon shrub, it's a hambush!"

§

Knowing how to properly use a guillotine
is certainly one way to get ahead.

§

Where do dead bricks go?
To the cementry.

§

I brought Emma to my office for
'Take Your Daughter to Work Day,'
but she was soon crying.
With my team watching, she explained:
"But, dad, where are all the clowns you work with?"

§

Why was Cinderella kicked off the soccer team?
She ran away from the ball.

§

I have my grandma on speed-dial.
We call it Instagram.

§

Why didn't the skeleton go trick or treating?
He had no body to go with him.

§

What do otters say when they get stuck in seaweed?
"Kelp! Kelp!"

§

What do you call a girl in the middle of a tennis court?
Annette.

§

It's difficult to say what my wife does.
She sells sea shells by the sea shore.

What happens to a bear's vision after dark?
He can bearly see.

§

I bought shoes from a drug dealer once.
I don't know what he laced them with,
but I was tripping all day.

§

A guy at work takes so much sick time to go to the dentist.
I'm betting he has her on retainer.

§

What sound does a 747 make when it bounces?
Boeing, Boeing, Boeing.

§

What's the difference between a cat and a comma?
One has claws at the end of its paws and
one is a pause at the end of a clause.

§

Puns make me numb, but math puns make me number.

§

Target has an exclusive new doll named Divorced Barbie.
She comes with all of Ken's stuff.

§

A man was caught stealing in a supermarket today
riding on the shoulders of a couple of vampires.
He was charged with shoplifting on two counts.

§

What do you call an alligator that wears a vest?
An investigator.

§

Did you hear about the red ship
that hit the blue ship on a clear day?
All of the sailors were purplexed.

§

Tired of looking at your smartphone?
There's a nap for that.

A woman wakes up in hospital:
"Doctor, Doctor, I can't feel my legs!"
"I'm sorry," replies the doctor,
"We had to amputate your hands."

§

Why did the bank hire a scientist who specializes in entomology?
He's an expert in fine ants.

§

Why did the man leave his socks on the golf course?
He had a hole in one.

§

Up next: How to sound good in a band.
Stay tuned.

§

My wife is nervous about talking to strangers
on our upcoming cruise.
I told her, "Don't worry. We're all in the same boat."

§

To whoever stole my copy of Microsoft Office, I will find you.
You have my Word.

§

What do you call a person who dislikes people with missing toes?
Lack-toes intolerant.

§

If dogs get cataracts, do cats get dogaracts?

§

My wife prefers the stairs,
whereas I always like to take the elevator.
I guess we are raised differently.

§

General: "How many troops do you have for today's operation?"
Captain: "483, sir."
General: "That'll do, round them up."
Captain: "500, sir."

CHAPTER 12

Two old men are sitting by a pool.
The first asks, "Have you read Marx?"
The other replies,
"Yes. I believe that comes from these chairs."

§

As I gave Dad his 60th birthday card he said to me:
"Just one would have been fine."

§

If you have 13 bananas in one hand
and 10 oranges in the other, what do you have?
Big hands.

§

I have this terrible condition
where I'm only happy while waiting in airports.
My doctor says it's terminal.

§

Did you read about the bakery that burned down?
Their whole business is now toast.

§

What do you get when you cross the Atlantic with the Titanic?
About half-way.

§

What did the right eye say to the other?
Between you and me, something smells.

§

I had to give up on my idea to create a miniature flamethrower.
It was burning a hole in my pocket.

§

What does a priest say at the end of the service to rid the church
of bugs? Let us spray.

§

Evidently, I snore so loudly
that it scares everyone on the bus I'm driving.

England doesn't have a kidney bank,
but they do have a Liverpool.

§

Singing in the shower is all good fun
until shampoo and body wash get in your mouth.
Then it's a soap opera.

§

After my wife started cancer treatment and we lost our home,
the health department's discovery of mold in my bakery
is the yeast of my worries.

§

Why did the coffee no longer feel safe at home?
It was mugged.

§

I tried looking up ice cream puns on the internet.
Then my browser froze.

§

I couldn't understand why my brother
worked at the largest mint on the planet.
Now, it makes all the cents in the world.

§

I've applied to work at Apple and BlackBerry.
But so far, my efforts have been fruitless.

§

I broke my finger today.
But on the other hand I'm fine.

§

My crush finally agreed to go on a date
after I opened a bottle of tonic water.
You could say I Schwepped her off her feet.

§

What do you call a green onion with mad rhyme skills?
A rapscallion.

§

On our last cruise, I stopped in an island voodoo shop
and immediately punched a laughing psychic.
My mother always told me to strike a happy medium.

How do phones get married?
They give each other a ring.

§

What's the most British fruit in the world?
The bloody orange.

§

I got my best friend a refrigerator for her birthday.
I can't wait to see her face light up when she opens it.

§

How did the hipster burn his tongue?
He drank coffee before it was cool.

§

I hate seeing my loved ones go.
It's even worse with fives, tens, and twenties.

§

What did the grape say when the elephant stepped on it?
Nothing, it just gave out a little wine.

§

For the pachydermist at the zoo,
if it isn't about elephants,
it's irrelephant.

§

My grandpa's last words were:
"It's worth spending a little extra for good speakers."
That was some sound advice.

§

How many pragmatists does it take to change a light bulb?
One.

§

There's really no point in using dull knives.

§

I often imagine what Benjamin Franklin's
opinion would be on current issues.
He's usually on the money.

CHAPTER 13

Why couldn't the amputee find work as an editor?
He didn't have the footage.

§

Can vegans eat pudding? No!
How can you have any pudding if you don't eat your meat?

§

Smokey the Bear reminds us to never buy flowers from a monk.
Only you can prevent florist friars.

§

I haven't slept for three days.
That would be far too long in bed.

§

What kind of music do balloons hate the most?
Pop.

§

Why are fish usually really easy to weigh?
Because most have their own scales.

§

I ordered a chicken and an egg from Amazon.
I'll let you know.

§

How many times does the exaggeration club meet weekly?
About a million.

§

My uncle stores his coin collection in Altoids tins.
He claims it keeps them in mint condition.

§

What do you call sour cream that has traveled the world?
Cultured.

§

My mom gets upset whenever I mess with her red wine.
Yesterday, I added fruit and sparkling water
and now she's sangria than ever.

"Dad, what does entropy mean?"
"Well, son, it's hard to say.
It isn't what it used to be."

§

I'm reading a book about zero gravity chambers.
I can't put it down.

§

How many surrealists does it take to change a light bulb?
Two: one to do it and another to melt a clock.

§

I had a disturbingly long dream that I was making a Caesar salad.
I was tossing all night.

§

I accidentally glued my autobiography to my hand,
but nobody seems to believe me.
That's my story, and I'm sticking to it.

§

The other day my wife asked to pass her lipstick,
but I passed her a glue stick.
She isn't talking to me right now.

§

Did you hear about the dyslexic, agnostic insomniac?
He lies awake at night wondering if there is a dog.

§

A square and a circle walk into a pub.
The square says to the circle:
"Your round."

§

Ancient astronomers were bored watching the earth turn,
so after 24 hours, they called it a day.

§

What's the difference between
the largest plane and the largest planet?
1t.

§

Bouncer: "I'm going to have to ask you to leave."
Me: "Why?"
Bouncer: "I have no idea who you are and this is my trampoline."

Where does a mansplainer get his water?
From a well, actually.

§

My grandfather was his battalion's mime during WWII.
He doesn't talk about it.

§

Ever tell a good steak pun?
You should, it's a rare medium well done.

§

Ladies, if he can't appreciate your fruit jokes,
you need to let that mango.

§

Did you read about the Spanish high speed train robbery?
They say the robber had a loco-motive.

§

How does a dinosaur pay its bills?
With Tyrannosaurus checks.

§

Did you hear about the poor man whose blanket slipped off his
hospital bed just before he was about to be discharged?
He never recovered.

§

I've started a small business building boats in my attic.
Sails are going through the roof.

§

My son tried to change the time.
But not on my watch.

CHAPTER 14

I used to hate facial hair.
But then it grew on me.

§

What creature is smarter than a talking parrot?
A spelling bee.

§

After months of wanting a light purple marker at work,
I finally found one.
It was the highlight of my day.

§

What did the policeman say to his belly?
"You're under a vest."

§

When taking a calculus exam,
make sure you don't sit between identical twins.
It's difficult to differentiate between them.

§

What do you call a taxi made out of vegetables?
A corn on the cab.

§

Do you know what happened to the turkey?
He didn't Czech his flight plans and ended up in Greece.
Unfortunately, people were Hungary.

§

It's tricky knowing when to take the tea bag out.
There's a steep learning curve.

§

What's the difference between unlawful and illegal?
One's against the law, the other is a sick bird.

§

To be Frank, I'd have to change my name.

My Indian friend announced to her family
she wants to wear a ball gown to her wedding.
She told them:
"Sorry, but not Sari."

§

Why do bees stay inside their hives all winter?
Swarm.

§

My friend wouldn't stop telling me bird puns.
Little did he know, toucan play at that game.

§

What do you call a wild American bison that lifts weights?
A buff-alo.

§

Almost a dozen bugs were wandering outside my door,
so I made a small paper house for them.
I guess that makes me their landlord and them my tenants.

§

I wanted to become a conductor.
But there was too much training.

§

As an earthquake shook their barn,
one horse turned to another and asked,
"Do you think this place is stable?"

§

Unbelievable! 364 Days until Christmas,
and there are decorations everywhere already.

§

I'm trying to organize a hide and seek tournament,
but I'm having a lot of trouble.
Good players are hard to find.

§

My friend hates when I make jokes about his weight.
He needs to lighten up.

§

If you cut down a pine tree in the forest,
but it doesn't understand why,
is it just stumped?

Why is the ocean salty?
Because the shore never waves back.

§

Why did the winemaker have a nervous breakdown?
He couldn't bottle it up any more.

§

Did you know that a group of crows is known as a fatality?
Well, technically it's murder if there's probable caws.

§

My grandfather died because the
report said he had Type AB blood.
Unfortunately it was a Type-O.

§

Did you hear about the guy whose entire left side got cut off?
He's all right now.

§

My son's math teacher called him average.
I really think that's mean.

§

I want to die peacefully in my sleep like my grandfather.
Not screaming and yelling like his passengers.

§

How much does a millennial weigh?
An instagram.

§

On Monday, a delivery van with
files and filing cabinets was stolen.
Tuesday, another with clear buckets and
labeled boxes was stolen.
The police believe it was organized crime.

§

Why did the horses get a divorce?
They didn't have a stable relationship.

CHAPTER 15

The first computer dates back to the Garden of Eden.
It was an Apple with limited memory, just one byte.
Then everything crashed.

§

I had a game of quiet badminton today.
It's like regular badminton but without the racket.

§

Did you know about the explosion at the toilet paper factory?
Many experienced soft tissue damage.

§

What's a vegetarian zombie's favorite food?
A human bean.

§

When I was younger,
I felt like a man trapped inside a woman's body.
Then I was born.

§

Why couldn't the duck cross the road?
Because he got his foot stuck in a quack.

§

My grandma used to feed me alphabet soup.
I hated it, but she thought I liked it.
She was just putting words in my mouth.

§

Why was the ice cream bad at tennis?
It had a soft serve.

§

What's Michelle Obama's favorite vegetable?
Barackoli.

§

One should never iron a four leaf clover.
You don't want to press your luck.

Did you hear about the invisible man
who married an invisible woman?
Their kids aren't much to look at either.

§

My wife bought me a sweater that was picking up too much static.
I went back to exchange it.
They replaced it, free of charge.

§

I may try to use contractions more often,
but it can get confusing.
Maybe I won't, maybe I'll.

§

Shout out to the people who are wondering
what the opposite of in is.

§

What do you say to your sister when she's crying?
"Are you having a crisis?"

§

Mark Hamill made a lot of money for
his role as Skywalker in Star Wars.
One might say it was Lucrative.

§

A limbo champion walked into a bar.
He was disqualified.

§

My wife loves our cats,
but they don't seem to care about her.
The feline's not mutual.

§

Why is dark spelled with a 'k' and not a 'c'?
Because you can't see in the dark.

§

My new boss reprimanded me for asking customers
if they preferred smoking or non-smoking.
Technically, the correct terms are cremation or burial.

§

I just can't trust trees.
They seem kind of shady.

My friend bet me $50 that I couldn't build a car out of spaghetti.
You should've seen the look on her face as I drove pasta.

§

I read recently there's been an increase in
crime in high rise apartment buildings.
That's wrong on so many levels.

§

Jokes about communism aren't funny
unless everyone gets them.

§

Right before interrogation, the man says:
"I'm not saying a word without my lawyer present."
Police: "You are the lawyer."
Lawyer: "Exactly, where's my present?"

§

I'm open to trying all kinds of art.
Still life is where I draw the lime.

§

You don't understand cloning?
Don't worry.
That makes two of us.

§

What do you call a centenarian with excellent hearing?
Deaf defying.

§

I'm teaching my son to tell jokes about the post office.
His latest ones have my stamp of approval.

§

The only thing some of my friends like doing with me is eating.
I call them my taste buds.

§

I don't trust stairs.
They're always up to something.

§

What do you call a person with one arm and no legs?
By their name; don't be a jerk.

CHAPTER 16

After trying new cheese at the grocery store,
the clerk asked for my feedback.
I told him it tasted grate.

§

The original draft of Toy Story 4
had a scene where Woody's friends died.
They cut it because it was too much of a buzzkill.

§

Recently, I was asked if I could perform under pressure.
I said I'd try but I know all the words to Bohemian Rhapsody.

§

What happened to the currency exchange on the volcano?
It went bank-erupt.

§

How many psychiatrists does it take to change a light bulb?
Only one, but the light bulb has to want to change.

§

Do old men typically prefer boxers or briefs?
Depends.

§

I'm color blind, but I swear I could see purple today.
Sadly, it was only a pigment of my imagination.

§

What has more courage, a creek or the rock in it?
A rock, because it's a little boulder.

§

What is the fastest beverage on earth?
Milk.
It's pasteurized before you even see it.

§

Why do bicycles fall over so often?
Because they're two-tired.

If I had a dollar for every girl that didn't find me attractive,
eventually they would find me attractive.

§

Someone was giving away dead batteries
at a garage sale this weekend.
They were free of charge.

§

Before you criticize someone, walk a mile in their shoes.
Then when you do criticize them,
you'll be a mile away and have their shoes.

§

What was the pickle's favorite game show?
Dill or No Dill.

§

I made fish tacos last night, my best yet.
Sadly, they ignored them and swam away.

§

Nine months isn't really that long,
it only feels like a maternity.

§

Our math professor was over half an hour late to his first class,
sixteen minutes late to his second,
and eight minutes late to the last.
At this rate, he'll never be in class on time.

§

What do you call a hundred centipedes?
A dollarpede.

§

I just quit my job as a scuba diving instructor.
Deep down, I realized it wasn't for me.

§

What do you call someone with no body and no nose?
Nobody knows.

§

An unspeakable thing happened to me at work today.
Let's not talk about it.

Nurse: "There's a patient at the front desk
who says he's invisible."
Doctor: "Just tell him I can't see him right now."

§

If someone finds my lost glasses,
I hope they contact me.

§

I'm reading a horror story in Braille.
Something bad is going to happen,
I can feel it.

§

My uncle had the heart of a lion.
And a lifetime ban from the zoo.

§

My son took the bus home by himself
and I'm pretty disappointed.
He left it blocking our driveway.

§

What do you call a sleeping bull?
A bulldozer.

§

Before I stated lifting weights,
I used to hate my physique.
Now my muscles are really growing on me.

§

Why is there justice in a signed confession?
The criminal must write their wrongs.

§

The first French fries where not actually made in France.
They were made in grease.

§

I joined a Lord of the Rings secret society
and just learned the secret sign.
It's a Tolkien gesture.

VOLUME III

CHAPTER 17

What type of doctor provides treatment
at any time of day or night?
An oncall-ogist.

§

Atheism is a non-prophet organization.
Agnosticism needs a better bookkeeper:
it doesn't know whether it has a prophet or not.

§

I feel bad for the grim reaper's dentist.
He frequently brushes with death.

§

How did the Mexican army keep warm
during the Battle of the Alamo?
They used chicken fa-heat-us.

§

We lost 25% of our roof in that last big hurricane.
Oof!

§

Why was the cow so aggressive?
It was in a bad moood.

§

Which weighs more:
a pound of bricks or a pound of feathers?
Feathers.
You have to carry the weight of what you did to the poor birds.

§

The best way to get someone to fall for you is by tripping them.

§

What's the difference between a hippo and a zippo?
One's pretty heavy and the other is a little lighter.

I decided to become a math teacher.
I'll focus on teaching subtraction;
I just want to make a difference.

§

What do you call a pig with three eyes?
A piiig.

§

At first I didn't understand how a computer mouse worked.
But then it just clicked.

§

Don't you hate it when a teacher lies,
saying the homework will be a piece of cake?
It always tastes like paper.

§

There are basically three kinds of people in the world.
Those who can count and those that can't.

§

Why were Star Wars 4-6 released before 1-3?
Because in charge of the schedule Yoda was.

§

Did you hear the new pop song about a tortilla?
Well, it's more of a wrap really.

§

Why are combs good presents for bald people?
It's a gift they'll never part with.

§

A horse walks into a pub, bartender says: "Hey!"
The horse replies:
"Neigh. But I'll take some Quick Oats for the road."
The asphalt in the corner says: "Thanks."

§

Every room has to have a door,
and that's where I come in.

§

I'm pretty sure that the hotel receptionist was checking me out.

Did you know janitors created a weightlifting exercise?
They call it the power clean.

§

What is a mathematician's preferred type of toilet paper?
Multiply.

§

I went to the zoo today but for all of the exhibits and habitats,
they only had one animal, a dog.
It was a shih tzu.

§

Why is 5am like a pig's tail?
Because it's twirly!

§

How does a penguin build its house?
Igloos it together.

§

What do you call a queue of rabbits losing their fur?
A receding hareline.

§

What do you call a genetically engineered cow?
A mootant.

§

I asked my neighbor if he would tell me =
how often he cuts his lawn.
He says it's on a need to mow basis.

§

Why do electrical repairmen make the best journalists?
They're always investigating current events.

§

Before surgery, my anesthetist offered to
knock me out with gas or a boat paddle.
It was an ether/oar situation.

§

A young boy swallowed some pennies
and was taken to the hospital.
His father rushed over and asked how he was.
The nurse replied:
"No change yet."

CHAPTER 18

Did you hear that all of the toilets were stolen from NYPD HQ?
The detectives have nothing to go on.

§

My wife is furious at our next door neighbor
for sunbathing in her backyard.
Personally, I'm on the fence.

§

I ate my old Apple watch last week.
I had difficulty passing time.

§

My son asked me what our home IP address was.
I pointed to the toilet.

§

I saw a friend of mine sweep a girl off her feet.
He's quite the aggressive janitor.

§

Why did the tomato blush?
Because it saw the salad dressing.

§

Everyone loves my tattoos and asks where I had them done.
No one believes when I tell them Spain.
Nobody expects the Spanish ink precision.

§

Helpful advice if you're ever attacked by a group of killer clowns:
Go for the juggler.

§

How does Mike Tyson think the unthinkable?
With an itheberg.

§

Despite the current fad, I regret rubbing ketchup on my eyes.
But that's Heinz sight for you.

Growing up, I always thought a prima donna was
someone born before August 16, 1958.

§

Why did the cookie go to the doctor?
He was feeling crummy.

§

A group of competitive chess players were
kicked out of a hotel lobby for discussing their wins.
The manager didn't want chess nuts boasting in an open foyer.

§

What do you call a fish without an eye?
Fsh.

§

How do you give a waterbed more bounce?
Fill it with spring water.

§

They have a toothless grizzly at the zoo.
Biggest gummy bear you'll ever see.

§

My son is obsessed with everything Star Wars.
This week, he's also into cars.
I bought him a toy Yoda.

§

What's the difference between a pedant and a kleptomaniac?
One takes things literally and the other takes things, literally.

§

I asked the store clerk where to find the Terminator DVDs.
He responded, "Aisle B, Back."

§

Job recruiter:
"Tell me about your dream employer. Boeing, Google, a startup?"
Me:
"Listening. Yes, I'd have to say that's my greatest weakness."

§

I wasn't going to get a brain transplant.
Then I changed my mind.

I, for one, like using Roman numerals.

§

I had a great joke about a blunt spear,
but I don't think there's any point.

§

Why can't you hear a pterodactyl use the washroom?
Because the 'p' is silent.

§

Not to brag, but I made six figures last year.
Unfortunately, they named me worst employee at the toy factory.

§

My friend turned 45 last week.
During an argument, I told tell her:
"Well, you're half right."

§

When my friend told me to stop pretending to be a flamingo
I had to put my foot down.

§

Good bakers use real butter
so that there is no margarine for error.

§

Welcome to plastic surgery addicts anonymous.
I see a few new faces here this week
and I must say I am disappointed.

§

Did the person who coined the term 'one hit wonder'
come up with any other phrases?

§

I was in a bar fight and shoved a guy into a light switch on the
wall.
He looked at me and said:
"Oh, it's on now!"

CHAPTER 19

A man goes to the vet about his dog's fleas.
The vet says: "I'm sorry; I'll have to put this dog down."
The man is shocked and asks why.
The vet replies: "Because he's too heavy."

§

Two guppies are in a tank,
one turns and says to the other:
"You shoot, I'll drive."

§

What's blue and not heavy?
Light blue.

§

What kind of duck is most easily seen on the Fourth of July?
The firequacker.

§

Do you know why I love rocks from old lake beds?
They're very sedimental to me.

§

Did you know that dogs can't read x-rays or MRIs?
But cats can.

§

I saw two security guards chasing someone
who had stolen a used board game.
It was trivial pursuit.

§

My friend Jay had twins recently and was
hoping to name them after him.
I suggested Kay and Elle.

§

How would the world operate if it were run by the Danish?
We would have a pastry-archal society.

§

What do peppers do when they're angry?
They get jalapeño face.

In Mother Russia, saunas were the place where
men made deals and debated politics.
Those were heated discussions.

§

Bartender asks a polar bear what he'd like to drink.
The polar bear hangs his head, sighs,
and finally says he'd like a beer.
The bartender asks, "Why the big paws?"

§

I once watched a video where a guy was electrocuted twice.
It was revolting.

§

What happens when you can't pay your exorcist?
You get repossessed.

§

What do you call a hot dog that won a race?
A wiener.

§

Woman: "Doc, my husband thinks he's a dog. Can you help?"
Psychiatrist: "Sure, have him lie down on the couch."
Woman says: "Oh no. He's not allowed on the couch."

§

Garbage collectors don't need formal education to get hired.
They pick it up as they go along.

§

Why did the pelican get kicked out of the restaurant?
He had a very big bill.

§

After my brother stole all the ice from my soda,
my mom asked what I wanted.
I replied: "Justice!"

§

What do you call a monkey in a minefield?
Baboom.

§

My dad really wanted me to make paper planes with him.
Eventually, I folded.

We all know that Albert Einstein was a genius,
but his brother Frank was a monster.

§

Started a new job and my fiancé
asked if there was a gym in the building.
I told her I wasn't sure;
I haven't met everyone yet.

§

I finally found work as a baker's assistant.
I really knead the dough.

§

Did you hear the news about the shovel?
It's ground breaking.
But the broom?
That really swept the nation.

§

What do you call a tree that you can hold in your hand?
A palm tree.

§

I'm absolutely terrified of swimming the English Channel.
It's one of my deepest fears.

§

A man turned to me and said:
"I built the Washington monument."
I replied:
"You raise a good point."

§

I was almost arrested for stealing cooking utensils.
It was worth the whisk.

§

Dad: "I can't believe you got me a house for my birthday!"
Son: "I hope you enjoy it. What are your plans?"
Dad: "I'm just going to live in the present."

§

I taught my son how to use the word abundance in a sentence.
He said: "Thanks Dad, that really means a lot."

CHAPTER 20

Did you hear about the dog that gave birth in the park?
She was cited for littering.

§

A customer walks into a bookstore and asks for a book on turtles.
Clerk: "Hardback?"
Customer: "Yes and their little heads pop in and out."

§

If you bought a DeLorean, would you drive it a lot,
or just from time to time?

§

What did the one legged man do at the ATM?
Check his balance.

§

I wanted to marry my English teacher when she got out of prison,
but apparently, you can't end a sentence with a proposition.

§

I told my wife to embrace her mistakes.
So she hugged me.

§

I decided to apply for Australian citizenship.
The interviewer asked:
"Do you have a criminal record?"
I replied:
"No. Is it still required?"

§

I built myself a voice-activated car.
I also have a regular car,
but that goes without saying.

§

My dad won't let me say 'hell,' so I asked,
"Have you thought of any alternative names for hell?"
He said: "I heaven't."

Did you read about the flat-earther
that attempted to walk to the edge of the earth?
He finally came around.

§

As a lumberjack, I'm proud to have cut exactly 2,000 oaks.
I know because every time I cut one, I keep a log.

§

What's the worst part about being a cross-eyed teacher?
You can't control your pupils.

§

A friend tried to steal hay but was caught and sent to jail.
I had to bale him out.

§

One time I paid $200 to see Prince in concert,
but I partied like it's $19.99.

§

Why was the Central American man shaky?
His condition was due to His-panic attacks.

§

Charles Dickens walks into a bar and orders a martini.
Bartender asks, "Olive or Twist?"

§

Well, you have to hand it to relay runners, right?

§

A cop at city hall told me some stories about tasers.
They were shocking.

§

My friend is making a lot of money
by selling photos of salmon wearing clothes.
It's like shooting fish in apparel.

§

Ranch dressing is just a fancy term for cowboy clothes.

§

I'm telling my friends about the benefits of eating dried grapes.
It's all about raisin awareness.

A scientist was developing an artificial eye.
A cynical blind man said it was impossible.
The scientist told him:
"You'll see."

§

When is a sandwich a chef?
When it's bakin' lettuce and tomato.

§

Me: "I'm afraid of planting an apple tree."
Neighbor: "Grow a pear."

§

I attempted a conversation with a sneaker.
He was very rude and told me to shoe.

§

I was confused when my wife gave me Play-Doh for my birthday.
I'm not sure what to make of it.

§

The cashier in my lane scanned
the eyes of a rude customer with her barcode reader.
The look on his face was priceless.

§

What type of tissue can you sleep on?
A nap-kin.

§

The pastor asked the congregation
to skip the hymn's fourth verse.
They refrained.

§

What word becomes shorter when you add two letters to it?
Short.

§

You can't run through a camp site.
You can only ran because it's past tents.

§

I was accused of being a plagiarist.
Their word, not mine.

CHAPTER 21

Did you hear about the Buddhist monk
who refused to have his mouth numbed at the dentist?
He wanted to transcend dental medication.

§

Want to hear a joke about a stone?
Never mind, I'll just skip that one.

§

What did the clock do when it was hungry?
It went back four seconds.

§

Why are mountain ranges funny?
Because they're hill areas.

§

I found a pencil with two erasers in the clearance section.
Now I can see why.
It was pretty pointless.

§

Three men walked into a bar.
They all said ouch.

§

The amount of cabbage is directly proportional
to the square root of the carrots
divided by the volume of the mayo.
That's Cole's Law.

§

Why do chemists make excellent conflict resolution therapists?
Because they always have a good solution.

§

I'm tired of people coming to my door
saying I need to be saved or I'll burn.
Annoying firefighters.

§

How are dog catchers paid?
By the pound.

Did you hear about the butcher
who accidentally backed into his meat grinder?
He got a little behind in his work.

§

I used to work in a grenade factory.
It was so quiet that you could hear a pin drop.

§

If your parachute doesn't deploy,
you have the rest of your life to fix it.

§

I like the sound of 'fiancé.'
It has a ring to it.

§

A woman wasn't sure she could afford an attorney so she asked:
"Will you answer two questions for $500?"
He responded:
"Absolutely! What's the second question?"

§

Why should you never take offense?
Because your neighbor's dogs might run right into your garden.

§

I wondered why the baseball was getting bigger.
Then it hit me.

§

My coworker asked me to bring something hard to write on.
I'm not sure why she's mad;
it's pretty hard to write on sand.

§

What's the longest word in the dictionary?
Smiles.
There's a mile between the two S's.

§

To call the whole Elon Musk controversy "Elon-Gate"
seems like a bit of a stretch.

§

Yesterday, a clown held a door open for me.
I thought it was a nice jester.

Did you hear about the criminal who was nutty as a fruitcake?
He was eventually given a trial by his pears.

§

Yesterday, I caught my girlfriend
out to dinner with her personal trainer.
I told her:
"This isn't working out."

§

I tried to impress someone by stepping on the pedal.
Turns out she'd seen a trash can open like that before.

§

What kind of pig should you ignore at a party?
A wild bore.

§

Why are foot injuries so serious?
Because they take so long to heel.

§

What did the family say when they called
the park service emergency support hotline?
Just bear with me here.

§

Do you know what happened to the cocky lion trainer at the zoo?
He was consumed by his own pride.

§

My dog is really good at playing fetch.
I think I'll promote him to branch manager.

§

In chemistry class, our professor taught us that
covalent bonds are the strongest.
I always felt that Sean Connery was the strongest Bond.

§

What did the scarf say to the hat?
You go on ahead;
I'm going to hang a bit longer.

CHAPTER 22

A sausage and an egg are in a frying pan.
The sausage complains to the egg about the heat.
The egg turns and says:
"Holy smokes! A talking sausage."

§

Mom: "We shouldn't curse around the kids anymore."
Dad: [puts the voodoo doll away]

§

How do you make a hot dog stand?
Take away its chair.

§

I asked the surgeon if I could administer my own anesthetic.
He said:
"Go ahead. Knock yourself out."

§

Once you've seen one shopping center,
you've seen the mall.

§

I bought an expensive laxative.
It gave me a good run for the money.

§

I used to be addicted to the hokey pokey.
Then I turned myself around.

§

I asked my high school girlfriend if I was the only one she's dated.
She said reluctantly said yes.
The others were at least sevens.

§

Guy: "You're the most average girl I've ever met."
Girl: "Wow, you're mean!"
Guy: "No, seriously, you are."

§

What are corals often stressing about the most?
Current events.

I'll never understand how people have a hard time sleeping.
It's so easy; I do it with both eyes closed.

§

No one believed me when I said
I can cut down large branches simply by looking at them,
but I saw it with my own eyes.

§

What do you call a hippie's wife?
Mississippi.

§

What do you call a fashionable lawn statue
with an excellent sense of rhythm?
A metro-gnome.

§

Did you know there is a church for the Eagles?
They are birds of pray, after all.

§

My aunt had a neck brace fitted years ago.
She's never looked back since.

§

Did you hear about the chameleon that couldn't change color?
It had a reptile dysfunction.

§

This afternoon before dinner,
I lined up my daughter's dolls by the window facing our grill.
I was preparing a Barbie queue.

§

What's the saddest thing you can put on your skin?
Disapp-ointment.

§

Farmers don't just grow grapes.
They're raisin them.

§

Not a fan of Orion's Belt, huh?
It truly is a big waist of space.

My mother in law doesn't like
the new stair lift we had installed for her.
She says it drives her up the wall.

§

Visiting the hospital for a broken thumb,
I asked the nurse if I'd be able to play the piano.
Nurse: "Yes, of course."
Me: "That's great, I couldn't play before."

§

Have you seen the new movie about the tractor?
Me neither I've only seen the trailer.

§

I caught a great documentary on beavers last night.
Best dam thing on TV.

§

How do retirees change light bulbs?
They don't.
They just tell you how great the last one was.

§

I wouldn't buy anything with Velcro.
It's a total rip-off.

§

What did the cannibal get when he showed up late for dinner?
The cold shoulder.

§

What's the difference between a step stool and a 3D printer?
The former is a ladder, while the latter is a former.

§

I don't know why dad jokes get a bad rap, women love them.
Otherwise they'd be bachelor jokes.

§

I really want to buy one of those grocery order dividers,
but the lady at the checkout keeps putting mine back.

CHAPTER 23

Why was the cheese deformed?
Because it was in bread.

§

Gandhi's feet were rough from walking barefoot.
He didn't eat much, making him frail.
Plus, his odd diet gave him bad breath.
He was a super callused fragile mystic plagued with halitosis.

§

My girlfriend and I watched three movies back to back.
Luckily, I was facing the TV.

§

A buddy of mine asked if I would pass along a
pamphlet from a political rally I was attending.
I told him yeah, brochure.

§

It's true, cats have nine lives.
But frogs croak every night.

§

Tell me one thing wrong with overstocking grocery shelves.
Go on. Aisle weight.

§

I was planning to make a joke about sodium and hydrogen,
but NaH.

§

A mushroom walks into a bar.
The bartender says to the mushroom:
"We don't serve your kind here."
Mushroom says: "But, I'm a fun-gi."

§

Why was the cantaloupe office staff so glum?
They were melon-colleagues.

§

What do you get when you cross a vampire with a snowman?
Frostbite.

My friend keeps telling me to cheer up.
He says it could be a lot worse:
I could be trapped inside a deep hole filled with water.
I know he means well.

§

Do the words 'well' and 'actually' each have only one syllable?
Well, yes, but actually, no.

§

I was going to tell a joke about spandex,
but it would've been a stretch.

§

Friend: "I have a new niece."
Me: "Why, was there something wrong with the old one?"

§

There is a fine line between a numerator and a denominator.
Only a fraction of people will understand.

§

What's orange and sounds like a parrot?
A carrot.

§

When we discovered that our French hotel was haunted, we left.
The place was giving us the crepes.

§

Where do oranges go to school?
The Navel Academy.

§

What's heavier, a gallon of water or a gallon of butane?
The water.
In any quantity, butane will always be a lighter fluid.

§

What do you call a dog that only eats ants?
An aardbark.

§

What type of music do wind turbines enjoy?
They're huge metal fans.

I have a machine that turns notes into dollar coins.
It makes no cents.

§

What do you call an army of marching babies?
An infantry.

§

My girlfriend has changed a lot since she became vegan.
It's like I've never seen herbivore.

§

Why is it so rare to see sheet music for violinists?
They usually play it by ear.

§

No matter your opinion of the police,
always call 911 if you see a tsunami.
They're huge emergent seas.

§

When your girlfriend comes home in a
white suit, smelling of honey, and covered in bee stings,
you know she's a keeper.

§

I started eating clocks on nights and weekends when I'm free.
It's a time consuming hobby.

§

As I sat in the chair,
my dentist asked if I had any questions before he got started.
I told him, no, I know the drill.

§

What do you call a square that was in an accident?
A wrecked angle.

§

A blind man walks into a bar.
And a chair, and a table, and some people.

§

Why do bees have sticky hair?
Because they use honeycombs.

CHAPTER 24

Did you read about the latest advances in pillowcase design?
They're making headlines.

§

I went into a pet shop and said:
"I would like a pet parrot for my daughter."
Confused, the owner replied:
"Sorry, we don't do swaps."

§

People are usually shocked when
they find out I'm not a very good electrician.

§

Did you hear about the guy selling defective chimps?
Don't worry, he offers a monkey-back guarantee.

§

What's big, gray, and makes you jump?
The elephant of surprise.

§

This past week we've tried teaching
our infant son how to hold things.
Sadly, he wasn't grasping the concept.

§

Someone asked if I was Russian.
I said no, I'm taking my time.

§

I invented a thought-controlled air freshener.
It makes scents when you think about it.

§

I generally use the self-checkout line when I grocery shop.
They always have the cutest cashiers.

§

Why do dogs have such a great attitude?
They like to stay paws-itive.

Why didn't they play cards on the Ark?
Noah was standing on the deck.

§

Why did the interior designer decorate the room
with fighter jets and biplanes?
The client requested plain wallpaper.

§

How do rhinos and elephants like their eggs?
Any way but poached.

§

How does a crow in Georgia communicate with a crow in Oregon?
Long distance caw.

§

Dad, that man accused you and Mom of
being something called pyromaniacs.
Is that true?
Yes, we arson.

§

Where do generals keep their armies?
In their sleevies.

§

I've often heard that 'icy' is the easiest word to spell.
Looking at it now, I see why.

§

Why is Batman in such a hurry?
He has to go to the Batroom.

§

Before I had weights, I used to work out by lifting cases of Coke.
I had to stop, because it was soda pressing.

§

What did baby computer call his father computer?
Data.

§

Why hasn't the sun gone back to school?
Because it already has a million degrees.

What do you call a deer with no eyes?
No idear.
What do you call a deer with no eyes and no legs?
Still no idear.

§

I have an addiction to cheddar cheese.
Don't worry, it's only mild.

§

Why did the engine have claustrophobia?
There wasn't much vroom to maneuver.

§

Robin: "Hey Batman, the Batmobile won't start."
Batman: "Did you check the battery?"
Robin: "What's a tery?"

§

What's a sea cow's favorite beverage?
Manatea.

§

It could be dangerous to drive my car right now.
But hey, bad brakes never stopped me before.

§

Why do cows have hooves instead of feet?
Because they lactose.

§

Do you want to hear a joke about notebooks?
Never mind, it's tearable.

§

Most people think T. rex couldn't clap
because they had short arms.
But really, it's because they're dead.

§

Why do the French only have a single egg at breakfast?
Because one egg is un oeuf.

VOLUME IV

CHAPTER 25

I can't stand perfume commercials.
They don't make any scents to me.

§

There are 10 types of people in the world.
Those who understand binary and those who don't.

§

I spent $300 on a limo and it didn't come with a driver.
I used all of my money and have nothing to chauffeur it.

§

I think the reason teen pregnancies are frowned upon is
that it's so much harder to give birth to a teenager.

§

My son asked why I was talking so quietly.
I said I was afraid Mark Zuckerberg was listening.
Son laughed, I laughed, Google Assistant laughed, Alexa laughed.

§

How many nihilists does it take to screw in a light bulb?
It doesn't matter.

§

Telemarketer: "Sir, would you like to
make a donation to the local orphanage?"
Dad: "Sure. Do you take boys or girls?"

§

When shopping for a vacuum cleaner,
check the reviews and pick the one that sucks the most.

§

Why is Peter Pan always flying?
He neverlands.

My uncle was the guy shot from a cannon at the circus.
When he retired, they had to close the show.
They couldn't find another man of his caliber.

§

I before E except after C has been disproven by science.

§

I was diagnosed as having a phobia of over-engineered buildings.
It's a complex complex complex.

§

What did one hat say to the other?
You stay here, I'll go on ahead.

§

My parents introduced my sister and me to minimalism.
It's the least they could do.

§

What part of the body is the last to die?
The pupils, they dilate.

§

In most cases,
cell phones won't crack when you accidentally drop them.

§

Last week, I joined a fancy gym and asked the trainer
what machine I should use to impress women.
He told me to try the ATM down the street.

§

A friend of mine tries to impress girls by
drawing realistic paintings of a Ford F-150.
He's a pickup artist.

§

What happens if a frog is caught parked in a loading zone?
It gets toad.

§

A man goes in a bar.
What's a mango doing in a bar?

§

Did you hear about the ruthless CEO that walked into the bar?
He ordered everyone around.

Shout out to my grandma.
That's the only way she can hear you.

§

My psychiatrist told me I'm incapable of describing my feelings.
Can't say that I'm surprised.

§

What did Batman say to Robin
after they loaded the Batmobile to respond to the Bat Signal?
"Robin, get in the car."

§

Smoking will kill you.
Bacon will kill you.
However, smoking bacon will cure it.

§

What is a pirate's favorite musical note?
The high C.

§

I was pulled over yesterday.
The officer asked if I had a police record.
I told him no, but I have a few of Sting's solo albums.

§

Why was the man fired from the Swedish fish factory?
He always took stock home.

§

What happens when your hot dogs get cold?
You get chili dogs.

§

Someone broke into my house last night and stole my limbo
trophy.
Really, how low can you go?

§

I was at a big house party last night.
There was a Slovak DJ, and a Czech one too.
A Czech one too.

CHAPTER 26

The waitress saw my leftovers and asked,
"Do you wanna box for that?"
I responded,
"No, but I'll arm wrestle any day."

§

Why can't an illegally parked car go on a toboggan run?
Because it only has one boot.

§

Why did the octopus beat the shark in a fight?
Because it was well armed.

§

I have a friend who really loves to count.
I wonder what he's up to?

§

If pronouncing 'V's like 'B's makes me sound Russian,
then Soviet.

§

A subatomic particle walks into a pub and says:
"Give me a beer."
The bartender says:
"Hey, Neutron! For you, no charge."

§

I just had my picture taken with REM.
That's me in the corner.

§

Where did Captain Hook get his famous hook?
A second hand store.

§

When is the best time of day to practice racket sports?
Tennish.

§

I just won't stand to listen to stereotypes anymore.
I always sit for Sony, Yamaha, or Bose.

Enjoying dinner at my favorite restaurant, the waiter asked,
"How did you find the steak?"
Me:
"I looked under the parsley."

§

At first I didn't like getting my hair cut short,
but it's starting to grow on me.

§

What did the monk say when returning to his monastery
after a trip across the globe?
The world is my cloister.

§

My wife returned from the store with the wrong type of cheese.
I'm sorry," she said.
I assured her: "It's all gouda."

§

How is the new furniture store doing?
Sofa so good!

§

At the store, I saw someone pouring soy sauce
on a guy on the floor.
I told him to stop immediately.
It's not right to Kikkoman when he's down.

§

I'm not sure if I like my new blender.
It keeps giving me mixed results.

§

Why is there no pain relief medication in the Caribbean?
Because parrots eat em all.

§

What did the manager say as he threw
Shakespeare out of his pub?
"You're Bard!"

§

Where do flat-earthers buy their clothes?
Lands' End.

What do they call the security patrols at the Samsung factory?
Guardians of the Galaxy.

§

Write the second to last letter of the alphabet on a piece of paper.
If you do it you'll see why.

§

My friend fell and told me that she couldn't stand up.
I said "Why not? It's a great movie!"

§

Why did the mail carrier quit his job?
He didn't like the post.

§

My physicist girlfriend told me that
she loves me to the moon and back.
I'm worried she means displacement, not distance.

§

When is a door not a door?
When it's a jar.

§

My kid didn't want to tell me that his tooth was loose.
I had to pull it out of him.

§

Two nuts are racing down the street.
One nut yells to the other: "I'm a cashew."

§

I once swallowed a dictionary.
It gave me thesaurus throat I've ever had.

§

Did you hear about the kleptomaniac
who had an accident in the laundromat?
He took a tumble.

§

Why did Waldo wear stripes?
He didn't want to be spotted.

§

I was going to give archery a shot,
but there are too many drawbacks.

CHAPTER 27

An atom walks into a bar and asks the bartender
if he's seen his missing electron.
"Are you sure she's missing?" asks the bartender.
"I'm positive," replied the atom.

§

At first I thought opening a shop
in the rain forest was a good idea.
Not so much, it's a saturated market.

§

I once tried to make a square but I ended up with an octagon.
That's what happens when you cut corners.

§

The burglars stole almost everything from our home.
I'm the most upset about our wardrobe mirror.
I just can't see myself without it.

§

Why did the investigative journalist quit her job?
She didn't like the post.

§

Did you hear about the mathematician
who's afraid of negative numbers?
He'll stop at nothing to avoid them.

§

I recently took a pole at my sister's outdoor wedding.
I discovered that 100% of people are angry when tents collapse.

§

Don't stare at a glass of water.
Take a pitcher it'll last longer.

§

What are the strongest days of the week?
Saturday and Sunday, the rest are weekdays.

§

Is it just me, or are circles pointless?

Capitalization can completely change a sentence.
Example: I like to eat candy vs. I like to eat capitalization.

§

After my trip to Ireland, I was inspired to name my horse Mayo.
And sometimes, Mayo neighs.

§

Scientists have conclusively determined
the leading cause of dry skin.
Towels.

§

My friend was electrocuted yesterday.
He tried to eat an Apple.

§

My furniture and I are really close.
I go way back with my recliner.

§

What did the big plate say to the teacup?
Lunch is on me.

§

I recently watched a documentary on how
the Titanic's hull was put together.
It was riveting.

§

What pet is furry, needs occasional cleaning,
but never needs feeding?
Carpet.

§

Did you hear about the guy who flew so close to the sun
that he touched it at exactly one point?
He was a real tan gent.

§

How do you find Will Smith in the snow?
Look for fresh prints.

§

What do you call a cow with only two legs?
Lean beef.

What happens to famous composers after they die?
They decompose.

§

I had a dream that I was a muffler last night.
I woke up exhausted.

§

What do you call a small bridge that has trouble concentrating?
A really short tension span.

§

How do ants avoid the flu?
They have anty bodies.

§

I saw an ad that read:
"Bose stereo for sale, $5, volume stuck at 11."
I thought to myself:
"I can't turn that down!"

§

It's been a month since I sent my hearing aid in for repairs.
I've heard nothing since.

§

Every morning at breakfast,
I tell my family that I'm going for a jog,
and then I don't.
It's my longest running joke of the year.

§

What is a dog's favorite car modification?
A sub-woofer.

§

Scientists have grown human vocal cords on mice in a lab.
The results speak for themselves.

§

I was arrested for stealing people's electrons.
I was heavily charged, despite my victims saying
it was an overall positive experience.

CHAPTER 28

Did you hear about the pelican with a successful standup career?
His jokes really fit the bill.

§

I'd like to attend my friend's Punjabi wedding
but I wasn't invited.
I hear it's going to be Sikh,
but it's naan of by business.

§

My wife was clearing the table.
She asked if I was done with the glasses.
I told her no, I need them to see.

§

Why didn't the clam share his candy?
Because he was shellfish.

§

My wife insists I'm the cheapest man in the world.
I'm not buying it.

§

I wanted to buy camouflage pants from the army surplus store
but I couldn't find any.

§

Did you hear about the latest tropical fruit diet?
These fads are enough to make a mango crazy.

§

A magician was driving down the highway.
All of a sudden he turned into a driveway.

§

My wife moved to the West Indies.
Jamaica?
No, she left of her own free will.

§

6:30 is my favorite time.
Hands down.

What's the difference between roast beef and pea soup?
You can roast beef but you can't pea soup.

§

I bought a coffee table but I might send it back.
It tastes nothing like coffee.

§

MI6:
"You're under arrest for stealing all of Wikipedia's servers."
Me:
"Wait! I can explain everything."

§

Why didn't the teddy bear finish its dinner?
It was stuffed.

§

I almost got caught stealing a board game today.
But it was a risk I was willing to take.

§

My friend wanted me to take care of his
extremely fragile pumpkin.
I assured him that I would gourd it with my life.

§

What did one triplet say to the others?
We're running out of womb!

§

My son beat my neighbor in a marathon.
He's now in custody for assault.

§

I told my son I was named after Thomas Jefferson.
He said, "But dad, your name is Brian."
I said, "I know, but I was named AFTER Thomas Jefferson."

§

What do you call two guys hanging above a window?
Kurt and Rod.

§

If you have bladder problems, urine trouble.

My psychologist told me that my
addiction to exhibitionism is incurable.
I'll show her.

§

Banks should really learn to keep their ATMs stocked.
I tried four different ones and each said insufficient funds.

§

I was out with my young daughter and ran into an old friend.
"This is Beth," I said, introducing my kid.
"What's Beth short for?" he asked.
"Well, she's only four."

§

What do you get when you cross a dinosaur with a firecracker?
Dino-mite.

§

Want to hear a joke about planes?
Never mind, it's over your head.

§

Always remember the best angle to approach a problem from:
the try-angle.

§

I found a nickel on the ground and
I have a feeling I'm going to find a penny later.
It's my sixth sense.

§

Son: "How did you sleep last night?"
Dad: "I closed my eyes and waited."

§

My wife and I are planning a trip to
San Francisco to see the Golden Gate.
She asked what I was going to do when we see it.
I suggested we cross that bridge when we get there.

§

My wife suggested I write a book based on all of my silly jokes.
I thought that was a novel idea.

CHAPTER 29

On a family trip to Arizona, my son complained about
the oppressive 113 degree heat.
I suggested he walk to the corner where it's 90 degrees.

§

What do Alexander the Great, Erik the Red,
and Winnie the Pooh have in common?
Same middle name.

§

What do you call a group of gangsters that
refuse to turn off the lights on their cameras?
A flash mob.

§

What does a subatomic duck say?
Quark.

§

Hey, do you want to hear a construction joke?
Give me a second; I'm still working on it.

§

What's the difference between Prince William and a tennis ball?
One's heir to the throne and the other is thrown in the air.

§

Where's the best place to buy chicken broth in bulk?
The stock market.

§

The only thing that can defeat me is a double amputation.

§

A ship carrying artificial limbs
went down in the Bermuda Triangle.
All hands are reported lost.

§

My friends say I have a real gambling problem.
I bet I could go a week without stopping in the casino.

What is Mario's favorite clothing material?
Denim Denim Denim

§

What do you get when you wrap a cat in a blanket?
A purrrrito.

§

Why don't executioners typically high-five people?
They're used to leaving them hanging.

§

Did you hear about the restaurant on an asteroid?
Great food, no atmosphere.

§

Have you heard about the Spanish magician?
He said: "On the count of three, I will disappear! Uno! Dos!"
And then he vanished, without a tres.

§

And the best neckwear goes to...
Oh wait, it's a tie!

§

I was offered a job as an undertaker but I turned it down.
I couldn't dig it.

§

I was shocked when I found out my toaster isn't waterproof.

§

The giraffe says to the hippo,
"You know Joe the lion? Told me he's a shape shifter.
Can turn into any animal he wants."
The hippo scoffs:
"That guy? Nah, he's always lion."

§

I sold my fancy Dyson vacuum.
It was just collecting dust.

§

I watched a medical courier accidentally drop
an organ needed for transplant.
It was a heartbreaking scene.

There are so many bugs in my apartment that I called the police.
They're sending a swat team.

§

My friend is addicted to brake fluid.
However, he says he can stop any time.

§

Finding your lost luggage at the airport should be easy.
Unfortunately, that's just not the case.

§

Why was the broom late?
It overswept.

§

What's the difference between a thunderstorm
and a lion with a toothache?
One pours with rain and the other roars with pain.

§

On the first day of school,
I signed up for English, math, science, and geography.
The rest, as they say, is history.

§

What starts with e, ends with e, and only has one letter in it?
An envelope.

§

Don't tell secrets in corn fields.
Too many ears around.

§

How do you like your air?
I like my airplane.

§

A salad without condiments
is a problem that needs addressing.

§

German children are more likely to
share their toys than Americans
because German children are kinder.

CHAPTER 30

I loaded my favorite hiking playlist.
It has tracts from Peanuts, The Cranberries, and Eminem.
I call it my Trail Mix.

§

Why didn't the Indian baker make sourdough bread?
It's a naan starter.

§

How often should comedians tell chemistry jokes?
Periodically, as long as they get a reaction.

§

I used to work in a calendar factory.
I was let go because I took a couple of days off.

§

Does anyone know Bruce Lee's dad's name?
It's always been a Mr. Lee to me.

§

How long does it take to make a ton of butter?
An e-churn-ity.

§

Passing a psychic on my daily walk,
I decided to knock on her door for a session.
She asked, "Who's there?"
So I didn't bother.

§

What kind of murderer gets enough fiber?
A cereal killer.

§

My friend barely escaped injury after
falling through a plate glass window.
It must have been very paneful.

§

I can't take my dog to the pond anymore
because the ducks keep attacking him.
Guess that's what I get for buying a pure bread dog.

I have a pen that can write underwater.
It can write other words, too.

§

What happens when you drop a duck egg on the ground?
It quacks.

§

A long, horizontal line was being rude to me.
I said, "Wow, you've got some latitude."

§

When I was in college, I married my best friend.
My girlfriend at the time was upset,
but Josh thought it was hilarious.

§

What do you call a beehive without an exit?
Unbelievable.

§

I have a chicken-proof lawn.
It's impeccable.

§

I was just hired at the guillotine factory.
I'll beheading there soon.

§

Why was Pavlov's hair so soft?
Classical conditioning.

§

How many seconds are there in a year?
Twelve.
January 2nd, February 2nd...

§

Have you heard about the controversial new sunglasses?
They're extremely polarizing.

§

When does a bad joke turn into a dad joke?
When the punchline is apparent.

§

My doctor said my larynx is damaged and I may not speak again.
I can't tell you how upset I am right now.

After dinner my wife asked if I could clear the table.
I needed a running start, but I made it.

§

What's red and smells like blue paint?
Red paint.

§

I was embarrassed when my wife caught me
playing with my son's train set.
In a moment of panic, I threw a sheet over it.
I think I managed to cover my tracks.

§

I found out I'm allergic to horses.
It was destabilizing.

§

If you happen to catch a cold or flu,
spend a night in a smokehouse.
You'll be cured in no time.

§

My three favorite things are
eating my family and not using commas.

§

Time flies like the wind.
Fruit flies like a banana.

§

I was just informed that I've suffered amnesia since I was a teen.
You'd think I would remember something like that.

§

How many South Americans does it take to change a lightbulb?
A Brazilian.

CHAPTER 31

There was a massive explosion
at a cheese factory outside of Paris.
There was nothing left but debris.

§

To the man in the knee cast that stole my camouflage jacket:
You can hide but you can't run.

§

I couldn't do math in kindergarten
unless I was sitting in someone's lap.
It wasn't a problem,
but as an adult I can't count on anyone.

§

I got hit by a rental car.
It really Hertz.

§

A school of fish is in a large tank.
Unfortunately none of them know how to drive it.

§

What do you do with a dead chemist?
You barium.

§

My wife told me to take the spider out rather than kill it.
We got some drinks, cool guy.
He wants to be a web developer.

§

What do you give a terrier after they put on a good show?
A round of a-paws.

§

I put on a clean pair of socks each day of the week.
By Friday, I could hardly get my shoes on.

§

Last night, my wife dramatically ripped the blankets off of me.
Don't worry I recovered.

I saw a sign while driving that read:
"Watch for Children."
Sounds like a fair trade.

§

My deaf wife told me that "we need to talk."
That was not a good sign.

§

I originally invited my girlfriend to go to the gym
but texted that I got baseball tickets instead.
I hope she gets the message that we're not working out.

§

Why was the keyboard up all night?
It had two shifts.

§

Why did the phone wear glasses?
It lost all of its contacts.

§

What did the Italian sausage say to the German sausage?
You're the wurst!

§

I was able to get into an exclusive kite festival for free.
My friend pulled a few strings for me.

§

Can February March?
No, but April May.

§

Jim works the counter at a butcher shop.
He's six feet tall and wears a size 11 shoe.
What does he weigh?
Meat.

§

Me: "Alexa, I definitely don't use any other virtual assistant."
Alexa: "Are you Siri-ous?"

§

The recipe instructed to set the oven at 180 degrees.
The problem is I can't open the oven,
as its door now faces the wall.

I made a great joke at a mandatory meeting today.
You had to be there.

§

How does Sushi A usually greet Sushi B?
Wasabi.

§

Why can't you trust elements?
They make up everything.

§

What do you call a belt lined with watches?
A waist of time.

§

Why did the snail paint an 'S' on her car?
When she sped past, people would say:
"Look at that S car go!"

§

Buses stop at bus stations.
Trains stop at train stations.
My desk is a work station.

§

Queue is one letter followed by four silent letters.
They must be waiting their turn.

§

Say, Ernie, would you like some ice cream?
Yes, sherbert.

§

You ever just think, "Phuket?"
And book a last minute trip to Thailand?

§

Monks in a monastery fell on hard times and opened a fish fry.
On opening day, a woman saw one peeling potatoes:
"Hey, you must be the chip monk?"
He replied: "No, I'm a friar."

CHAPTER 32

Every morning after I wake up,
the first thing I do is make my bed.
Tomorrow I'm returning this piece of junk to Ikea.

§

Why do people like fizzy drinks?
They're sodalicious.

§

Mother: "Doc, all four of my boys want to be
valets as soon as they turn 16."
Doctor: "Ma'am, that's the worst case of
parking sons disease I've seen."

§

Why are possums considered marsupials?
They have the right koala-fications.

§

Did you read about the two men that stole a desk calendar?
They both got six months.

§

What kind of shoes do amphibians wear?
Open toad.

§

What do turtles and snails do on Sean Connery's birthday?
The shellebrate.

§

A son from a long line of wheat farmers decided to plant barley.
He was going against the grain.

§

I really should get on with my diet,
but I just have too much on my plate right now.

§

Let me make myself perfectly clear:
I wholeheartedly support every effort
to create a fully-functional invisibility cloak.

Who stole the goat stew from the Caribbean restaurant?
Curryminals.

§

My wife didn't believe me when I said that
I would give our daughter a silly name.
I decided to call her Bluff.

§

Why is it hard to trust Italian pasta?
Because some of them are spyghetti.

§

What do you call a pony with a sore throat?
A little hoarse.

§

The professor asked why she should grade on a curve.
I said, "This is calculus,
you could say that curves are integral to the class."

§

Why do cows have bells?
Because their horns don't work.

§

Did you hear about the dyslexic devil worshipper?
He sold his soul to Santa.

§

What do you get when you divide the
circumference of an orange gourd by its diameter?
Pumpkin pi.

§

Sherlock, what do they call primary school in America?
Elementary, my dear Watson.

§

I'll be in England soon and
I'm supposed to go to Greenwich a few weeks after I arrive.
Any ideas what to do in the meantime?

§

Do you know what really makes me smile?
My facial muscles.

Two parrots are sitting on a perch.
One says to the other, "Hey, do you smell fish?"

§

What do you call a pencil without lead?
Pointless.

§

What does a bodybuilder say when he runs out of protein?
No whey!

§

The devil told me he could play a mean fiddle.
I asked him demonstrate.

§

Why are Canadians so polite?
It's in their DN-Eh!

§

What do old people win for ageing?
Atrophy.

§

How did the metal frog greet his friends?
Rivet rivet.

§

I have a terrible fear of elevators.
I'm taking steps to avoid it.

§

Found out I was color blind the other day.
Boy that came right out of the orange.

§

What lies on the bottom of the ocean and shakes?
A nervous wreck.

§

Why did I want to be an editor, you ask?
Well, to cut a long story short.

FROM THE AUTHORS

So, yeah. Years ago, the genesis of the jokes... We didn't know, but a cascade of events would take us from devilishly charming unbridled singles to diaper changing, tantrum calming, homework assisting, bug killing dads (and moms).

Somehow we got from cruising the late night bar/club/festival scene to towing babies/toddlers/kids to happy hours with our supportive partners before rushing home to crash (hopefully after the kids). Along the way, corny (successful!) pickup lines morphed into dad jokes as we picked up a few responsibilities, lost a little hair, and added a few pounds/kilos.

Really, though, our jokes are for everyone. You don't have to be a dad (or mom) or even like kids (sometimes we don't!) to enjoy, obvs. We hope a bit of humour will brighten your days...

We hope you enjoy our jokes!

Stay up to date and join our community...
Plus watch out for more dad jokes and new titles!

Connect on social @1001dadjokes and on the web:

www.1001dadjokes.com

Printed in Great Britain
by Amazon

13421149R00059